WILLIAM'S DOLL

WILLIAM'S DOLL

by CHARLOTTE ZOLOTOW

pictures by WILLIAM PÈNE DU BOIS

■ HarperCollins*Publishers*

To Billy and Nancy

Text copyright © 1972 by Charlotte Zolotow
Pictures copyright © 1972 by William Pène du Bois
All rights reserved. Printed in Mexico.
Library of Congress Cataloging Card Number: 70-183173
ISBN 0-06-027047-0
ISBN 0-06-027048-9 (lib. bdg.)

William wanted a doll.
He wanted to hug it
and cradle it in his arms

and give it a bottle
and take it to the park
and push it in the swing

William wanted a doll.
He wanted to hug it
and cradle it in his arms

and give it a bottle
and take it to the park
and push it in the swing

and bring it back home
and undress it
and put it to bed

and pull down the shades
and kiss it goodnight
and watch its eyes close

and then
William wanted to wake it up
in the morning
when the sun came in

and start all over again
just as though he were its father
and it were his child.

"A doll!" said his brother.

"Don't be a creep!"

"Sissy, sissy, sissy!" said the boy next door.

"How would you like a basketball?"
his father said.
But William wanted a doll.
It would have blue eyes
and curly eyelashes
and a long white dress
and a bonnet
and when the eyes closed
they would make a little click
like the doll that belonged
to Nancy next door.
"Creepy" said his brother.
"Sissy sissy" chanted the boy next door.

And his father brought home
a smooth round basketball
and climbed up a ladder
and attached a net to the garage
and showed William
how to jump as he threw the ball
so that it went
through the net
and bounced down
into his arms again.
He practiced a lot

and got good at it
but it had nothing to do

with the doll.
William still wanted one.

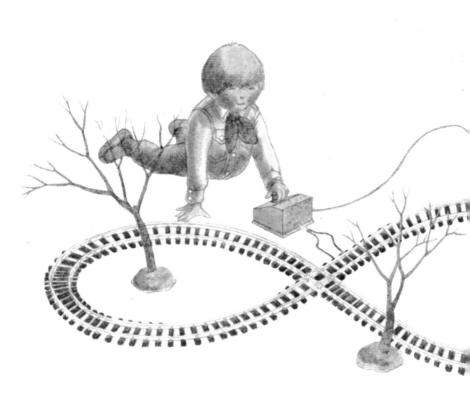

His father brought him an electric train.
They set it up on the floor
and made an eight out of the tracks

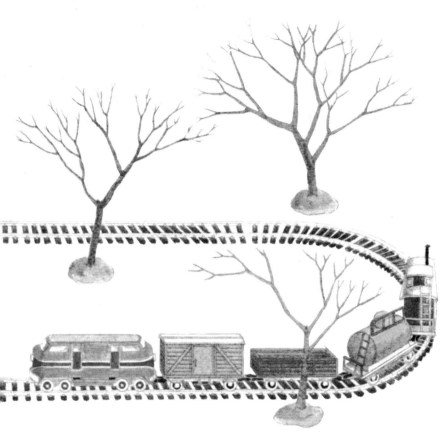

and brought in twigs from outside
and set them in clay
so they looked like trees.

The tiny train
threaded around and around the tracks
with a clacking sound.
William made cardboard stations

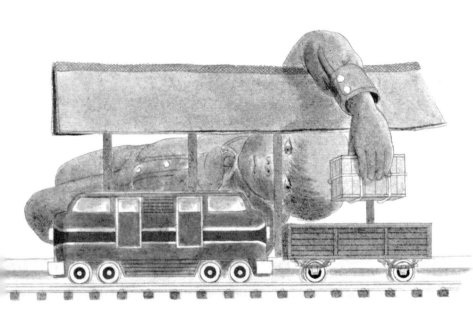

and tunnels
and bridges
and played with the train
a lot.

But he didn't stop wanting
a doll
to hug
and cradle
and take to the park.
One day
his grandmother came to visit.

William showed her
how he could throw the ball
through the net
attached to the garage outside.
He showed her the electric train
clacking along the tracks
through the tunnel
over the bridge
around the curve
until it came to a stop
in front of the station
William had made.

She was very interested
and they went for a walk together
and William said,
"but you know
what I really want
is a doll."
"Wonderful," said his grandmother.
"No," William said.
"My brother says
it will make me a creep
and the boy next door
says I'm a sissy
and my father
brings me
other things
instead."
"Nonsense," said his grandmother.

She went to the store and
chose a baby doll
with curly eyelashes
and a long white dress
and a bonnet.
The doll had blue eyes
and when they closed
they made a clicking sound
and William loved it
right away.

But his father was upset.
"He's a boy!" he said
to William's grandmother.
"He has a basketball
and an electric train
and a workbench
to build things with.
Why does he need a doll?"
William's grandmother smiled.
"He needs it," she said,
"to hug
and to cradle
and to take to the park
so that
when he's a father
like you,

he'll know how to
take care of his baby
and feed him
and love him
and bring him
the things he wants,
like a doll
so that he can
practice being
a father."